P9-DDI-113

ordinary

beast

ordinary

beast

P O E M S

nicole sealey

ecco
An Imprint of HarperCollins*Publishers*

ORDINARY BEAST. Copyright © 2017 by Nicole Sealey. All rights reserved. Printed in the United States of America. No part of this book may be used or reproduced in any manner whatsoever without written permission except in the case of brief quotations embodied in critical articles and reviews. For information, address HarperCollins Publishers, 195 Broadway, New York, NY 10007.

HarperCollins books may be purchased for educational, business, or sales promotional use. For information, please email the Special Markets Department at SPsales@harpercollins.com.

FIRST ECCO HARDCOVER EDITION

Designed by Suet Yee Chong

Library of Congress Cataloging-in-Publication Data has been applied for.

ISBN 978-0-06-268880-4

17 18 19 20 21   LSC   10 9 8 7 6 5 4 3 2 1

for my parents

for John

for you

for always.

contents

acknowledgments

I am grateful to the editors of the following publications where some of these poems, excerpts or versions of these poems, first appeared: The Academy of American Poets Poem-a-Day Series, *The Account*, *American Poetry Review*, *Best New Poets 2011*, Buzzfeed Reader, *Callaloo*, *Copper Nickel*, *Day One*, *The Feminist Wire*, *Literary Hub*, *Narrative*, *The New Sound*, *The New Yorker*, *No Tokens*, *Pinwheel*, *Ploughshares*, *Poetry International*, *Provincetown Arts Magazine*, *Stonecutter*, *Third Coast*, *Tupelo Quarterly*, *The Village Voice*, and *Washington Square Review*. With appreciation to Northwestern University Press, which published a selection of these poems in the chapbook *The Animal After Whom Other Animals Are Named*.

Huge thanks to Ecco's Bridget Read and Allison Saltzman for putting up with me, and my editor Daniel Halpern for believing in this work. With lots of love to my ride-or-die first readers: John Murillo, Petra Martin, and Martha Collins. Deep gratitude to my teachers: Chris Abani, Catherine Barnett, Andrea Cohen, Toi Derricotte, Cornelius Eady, Kimiko Hahn, Yusef Komunyakaa, Deborah Landau, Marilyn Nelson, Willie Perdomo, Sharon Olds, Alan Shapiro, and Patricia Smith. Thank you to friends who read poems from *Ordinary Beast* before there was an *Ordinary Beast*: Jericho Brown, Naomi Jackson, Tyehimba Jess, Rickey Laurentiis, Roger Reeves, and Metta Sáma.

Shout-outs to my comrades at Cave Canem and my classmates at NYU for their suggestions and support. Neal Thompson and Katie Raissian, your generosity knows no bounds.

Many thanks to the following institutions, without which I would not have had the resources to complete this collection: Atlantic Center for the Arts, Cave Canem Foundation, Community of Writers at Squaw Valley, Elizabeth George Foundation, Fine Arts Work Center in Provincetown, Hedgebrook, New York University's Graduate Creative Writing Program, the Poetry and Poetics Colloquium at Northwestern University, and the Poetry Project.

Lastly, dear reader, thank you.

ordinary

beast

medical history

I've been pregnant. I've had sex with a man
who's had sex with men. I can't sleep.
My mother has, my mother's mother had,
asthma. My father had a stroke. My father's
mother has high blood pressure.
Both grandfathers died from diabetes.
I drink. I don't smoke. Xanax for flying.
Propranolol for anxiety. My eyes are bad.
I'm spooked by wind. Cousin Lilly died
from an aneurysm. Aunt Hilda, a heart attack.
Uncle Ken, wise as he was, was hit
by a car as if to disprove whatever theory
toward which I write. And, I understand,
the stars in the sky are already dead.

a violence

You hear the high-pitched yowls of strays
fighting for scraps tossed from a kitchen window.
They sound like children you might have had.
Had you wanted children. Had you a maternal bone,
you would wrench it from your belly and fling it
from your fire escape. As if it were the stubborn
shard now lodged in your wrist. No, you would hide it.
Yes, you would hide it inside a barren nesting doll
you've had since you were a child. Its smile
reminds you of your father, who does not smile.
Nor does he believe you are his. "You look just like
your mother," he says, "who looks just like a fire
of suspicious origin." A body, I've read, can sustain
its own sick burning, its own hell, for hours.
It's the mind. It's the mind that cannot.

candelabra with heads

Had I not brought with me my mind
as it has been made, this thing,
this brood of mannequins, cocooned
and mounted on a wooden scaffold,
might be eight infants swaddled and sleeping.
Might be eight fleshy fingers on one hand.
Might be a family tree with eight pictured
frames. Such treaties occur in the brain.

Can you see them hanging? Their shadow
is a crowd stripping the tree of souvenirs.
Skin shrinks and splits. The bodies weep
fat the color of yolk. Can you smell them
burning? Their perfume climbing
as wisteria would a trellis.

as wisteria would a trellis.
burning? Their perfume climbing
fat the color of yolk. Can you smell them
Skin shrinks and splits. The bodies weep
is a crowd stripping the tree of souvenirs.
Can you see them hanging? Their shadow

frames. Such treaties occur in the brain.

Might be a family tree with eight pictured

Might be eight fleshy fingers on one hand.

might be eight infants swaddled and sleeping.

and mounted on a wooden scaffold,

this brood of mannequins, cocooned

as it has been made, this thing,

Had I not brought with me my mind

Who can see this and not see lynchings?

hysterical strength

When I hear news of a hitchhiker
struck by lightning yet living,
or a child lifting a two-ton sedan
to free his father pinned underneath,
or a camper fighting off a grizzly
with her bare hands until someone,
a hunter perhaps, can shoot it dead,
my thoughts turn to black people—
the hysterical strength we must
possess to survive our very existence,
which I fear many believe is, and
treat as, itself a freak occurrence.

legendary

I'd like to be a spoiled rich white girl.

VENUS XTRAVAGANZA

I want to be married in church. In white.
Nothing borrowed or blue. I want a white
house in Peekskill, far from the city—white
picket fence fencing in my lily-white
lilies. O, were I whiter than white.
A couple kids: one girl, one boy. Both white.
Birthright. All the amenities of white:
golf courses, guesthouses, garage with white
washer/dryer set. Whatever else white
affords, I want. In multiples of white.
Two of nothing is something, if they're white.
Never mind another neutral. Off-white
won't do. What I'd like is to be white
as the unsparing light at tunnel's end.

it's not fitness, it's a lifestyle

I'm waiting for a white woman
in this overpriced Equinox
to mistake me for someone other
than a paying member. I can see it now—
as I leave the steam room
(naked but for my wedding ring?)
she'll ask whether I've finished
cleaning it. Every time
I'm at an airport I see a bird
flying around inside, so fast I can't
make out its wings. I ask myself
what is it doing here? I've come
to answer: what is any of us?

happy birthday to me

....
....
....
....
....
....
....
....
....
....
....
....
....
....
....
....

What was I saying?—
Oh, yes. I don't mean
to be a bother, to burden
you with questions. But
did you know I wouldn't
last? That I would lose?
Had you asked, I could've
told you I'm not doing
especially well at being alive.

the first person who will live to be one hundred and fifty years old has already been born

[FOR PETRA]

Scientists say the average human
life gets three months longer every year.
By this math, death will be optional. Like a tie
or dessert or suffering. My mother asks
whether I'd want to live forever.
"I'd get bored," I tell her. "But," she says,
"there's so much to do," meaning
she believes there's much she hasn't done.
Thirty years ago she was the age I am now
but, unlike me, too industrious to think about
birds disappeared by rain. If only we had more
time or enough money to be kept on ice
until such a time science could bring us back.
Of late my mother has begun to think life
short-lived. I'm too young to convince her
otherwise. The one and only occasion
I was in the same room as the *Mona Lisa*,
it was encased in glass behind what I imagine
were velvet ropes. There's far less between

ourselves and oblivion—skin that often defeats
its very purpose. Or maybe its purpose
isn't protection at all, but rather to provide
a place, similar to a doctor's waiting room,
in which to sit until our names are called.
Hold your questions until the end.
Mother, measure my wide-open arms—
we still have *this much* time to kill.

in igboland

After plagues of red locusts
are unleashed by a jealous god
hell-bent on making a scene,
her way of saying *hello* or *how dare you*,
townspeople build her a mansion
of dirt, embedded with bone china,
decorated wall-to-wall with statues
made from clay farmed from anthills—
statues of tailors on their knees
hemming the pant legs of gods;
statues of diviners reading
sun-dried entrails cast onto cloths
made of cowhide; statues of babies
breaching, their mothers' legs spread
wide toward the sky, as if in praise.

Sacrifices of goats and roosters
signal headway behind the fence
that hides the construction. A day is set.
Next spirit workers disrobe and race
to the fence, which they level, heap
into piles and set ablaze, so the offering
is first seen by firelight, not unlike

a beloved's face over candlelight.
The West in me wants the mansion
to last. The African knows it cannot.
Every thing aspires to one
degradation or another. I want
to learn how to make something
holy, then walk away.

legendary

You want me to say who I am and all of that?

PEPPER LABEIJA

What girl gives up an opportunity
to talk about herself? Not I. Not today.
I won't bore you with my biography—
just a few highlights from my résumé.
I don't aspire; I'm whom one aspires to.
The most frequently asked question isn't
WWJD? It's *what would Pepper LaBeija do*?
Really the question should be *what hasn't
she done*? I've been walking now two decades
and got more grand prizes than all the rest.
I hate to brag, but I'm a one-man parade,
Jehovah in drag, the church in a dress.
Outside these walls I may be irrelevant,
but here I'm the Old and the New Testament.

heretofore unuttered

As if god, despite his compulsions, were decent
and hadn't the tendency to throw off
all appearance of decorum, here I am
admiring this single violet orchid.
How lucky am I to go unnoticed
or so I imagine, when, at this writing,
there is a red-tailed hawk, somewhere,
tracking the soft shrills of newborn songbirds—?

a n d

Withstand pandemonium
and scandalous
nightstands
commanding candlelight

    and
    quicksand

and zinfandel
clandestine landmines
candy handfuls
and contraband

    and
    handmade

commandments
and merchandise
secondhand husbands
philandering

    and
    landless

and vandal
bandwagons slandered
and branded
handwritten reprimands

    and
    meander

on an island
landscaped with chandeliers
abandon handcuffs
standstills

    and
    backhands

notwithstanding
thousands of oleanders
and dandelions
handpicked

    and
    sandalwood

and mandrake
and random demands
the bystander
wanders

      in
      wonderland.

cento for the night i said, "i love you"

Today, gentle reader,

is as good a place to start.

But you knew that, didn't you? Then let us

give ourselves over to the noise

of a great scheme that included everything.

That indicts everything.

Let us roam the night together

in an attempt to catch the stars that drop.

White clouds against sky

come humming toward me.

One closely resembling the beginning

of a miracle. There's

the moonlight on a curved path

lighting the purple flowers of fragrant June.

I dreamed him and there he was

silent as destiny,

lit by a momentary match.

Men are so clueless sometimes,

like startled fish

living just to live.

We are dying quickly

but behave as good guests should:

patiently allowing the night

to have the last word.

And I just don't know,

you know? I never had a whole lot to say

while talking to strange men.

What allows some strangers to go past strangeness? Exchanging

yearning for permanence. And who wouldn't

come back to bed? Love—

How free we are; how bound. Put here in love's name:

called *John*. A name so common as

a name sung quietly from somewhere.

Like a cry abandoned someplace

in a city about which I know.

Like black birds pushing against glass,

I didn't hold myself back. I gave in completely and went

all the way to the vague influence of the distant stars.

I saw something like an angel

spread across the horizon like some dreadful prophecy

refusing to be contained, to accept limits.

She said, "Are you sure you know what you're doing?"

I love you, I say, desperate

to admit that

the flesh extends its vanity

to an unknown land

where all the wild swarm.

This is not death. It is something safer,

almost made of air—

I think they call it *god*.

Some say we're lucky to be alive, to have

a sky that stays there. Above.

And I suppose I would have to agree . . .

but the hell with that.

It isn't ordinary. The way the world unravels,

from a distance, can look like pain

eager as penned-in horses.

And it came to pass that meaning faltered, came detached.

I learned my name was not my name.

I was not myself. Myself

resembles something else

that had nothing to do with me, except

I am again the child with too many questions

as old as light. I am always learning the same thing:

one day all this will only be memory.

One day soon. For no good reason.

Dying is simple—

the body relaxes inside

hysterical light

as someone drafts an elegy

in a body too much alive.

Love is like this;

not a heartbeat, but a moan.

Can you see me

sinking out of sight

in the middle of our life?

Should I be ashamed of myself

for something I didn't know I—

(He walks by. He walks by

laughing at me.)

"What else did you expect

from this day forward?" *For better.* (Or worse.)

One life is not enough

to remember all the things

marriage is. This town at dawn

can will away my lust

to suck honey from the sunlight,

so why am I out here trying

to make men tremble who never weep?

After all's said and after all's done

and all arrogance dismissed,

the distance rumbles in

sparing only stars.

The moon, like a flower,

survives as opinion

making it almost transparent.

The pieces of heavy sky

heavy as sleep.

I close my eyes

and this is my life now.

    ***

virginia is for lovers

At LaToya's Pride picnic,
Leonard tells me he and his longtime
love, Pete, broke up.
He says Pete gave him the *house*
in Virginia. "Great," I say,
"that's the least his ass could do."
I daydream my friend and me
into his new house, sit us in the kitchen
of his three-bedroom, two-bath
brick colonial outside Hungry Mother Park,
where, legend has it, the Shawnee raided
settlements with the wherewithal
of wild children catching pigeons.
A woman and her androgynous child
escaped, wandering the wilderness,
stuffing their mouths with the bark
of chokecherry root.
Such was the circumstance
under which the woman collapsed.
The child, who could say nothing
except *hungry mother*, led help
to the mountain where the woman lay,
swelling as wood swells in humid air.

Leonard's mouth is moving.
Two boys hit a shuttlecock back and forth
across an invisible net.
A toddler struggles to pull her wagon
from a sandbox. "No," Leonard says,
"it's not a place where you live.
I got the *H In V. H I–*"
Before my friend could finish,
and as if he'd been newly ordained,
I took his hands and kissed them.

clue

i.

"Hands down, mustard
is the tastiest condiment," coughed Professor Plum—
his full mouth feigning hunger for the greens-
only sandwiches Mrs. White
laid out for Mr. Boddy's guests. Miss Scarlet
hadn't time to peel off her peacoat

before the no-frills food, which she declined, and a pre-cocktail
cocktail, which she accepted. Colonel Mustard
refused all fare, citing the risk of sullying his scarlet
and gold Marine Corps suit, then ate the sugarplums
that happenchanced his pockets like lint. Mrs. White
funneled the motley crew into the green-

house, where Mr. Green
was rumoring—his hand bridging his mouth to Mrs. Peacock's
ear in an effort to convince the white-
haired heiress that the sandwich-making maidservant must've
poisoned their plum
wine. Mr. Boddy's award-winning scarlet

runners initially amused Miss Scarlet,

the way one is amused by another with the same name. Mr. Green

thought it odd Mr. Boddy didn't show, told Professor Plum

as much. "Here we are, pretty as peacocks,

and our host is nowhere to be found," twirling his mustache

like the villain in a silent black and white.

Minutes into the conservatory tour, Mrs. White

introduced Mr. Boddy, who lay facedown in a scarlet-

berried elder. "This man," Colonel Mustard

said, "is dead. I know death, even when it's camouflaged by

greenery."

The discovery proved too much for Mrs. Peacock's

usual aplomb—

she fainted into the arms of Professor Plum.

When she came to, he appeared to her the way a white

knight would look to a distressed damsel. Semiconscious, Mrs.

Peacock

pointed to the deceased's pet Scarlet

Tanager perched on a lead pipe between the body and a briefcase

gushing green-

backs. Right away, Colonel Mustard

mustered up an alibi about admiring Mr. Boddy's plumerias.
Mr. Green followed suit with his own white-
washed version involving one Miss Scarlet and a misdemeanor plea
    copped . . .

ii.

"Dinner is served," said Mrs. White,
inviting Mr. Boddy's guests by their *noms de plume*
into the dining room for a precooked
reheated repast. Miss Scarlet
passed the pickings, which didn't pass muster,
to a rather ravenous Mr. Green.

Nobody faked affability better than Mr. Green,
waving his napkin like a white
flag, acting out the conquered in Colonel Mustard's
combat stories. Here was Professor Plum's
chance to charm a certain lady, catching what he called *scarlet*
fever. "I've seen more convincing peacocking

from a tadpole," quipped Mrs. Peacock,

retiring to the library, green

tea in hand and a tickled Miss Scarlet

in tow. Mr. Boddy's absence was so brazen it bred white

noise not even tales of exemplum

heroism, narrated by and starring Colonel Mustard,

could quiet—his presence, by all accounts, as keen as mustard

and showy as a pride of peacocks.

Like a boy exiled to his room, Professor Plum

excused himself, giving the others the green

light to do the same. Mrs. White

was in the kitchen scouring skillets

when she heard who she thought was Miss Scarlet

scream. Mr. Boddy's musty

old library was a crime scene, his final fall on this white-

knuckle ride towards death. "For the dead," Mrs. Peacock

said, "the grass is greener

on the side of the living." While plumbing

Mr. Boddy's body for clues, Professor Plum

found no visible wound—the would-be host appeared scarless,

despite blood haloing his head on the shagreen

rug and a bloodstained candlestick Colonel Mustard

recognized from dinner. Mrs. Peacock

avoided the sight, turning white

as the sheet with which Mrs. White covered the corpse. Plum

sick of the "poppycock" accusations, she sped into the starlit

night in a ragtop Mustang belonging to Mr. Green.

c u e

as

the

only

guest

accept
th is

poison

  same

                        as

                                                m   e

        in   duced

                                                                by

        a

        faint

                                distress

back   away

admiring

for

the
ravenous

a

fever

starring

a boy

who
scream   s
his final

sick
night

u n f u r n i s h e d

Something was said and she felt
a certain way about said something.
                          Certain only
that there was no mistaking the feeling
she felt—the sounds empty makes inside
a vacant house.

imagine sisyphus happy

Give me tonight to be inconsolable,
       so the death drive does not declare

itself, so the moonlight does not convince
       sunrise. I was born before sunrise—

when morning masquerades as night,
       the temperature of blood, quivering

like a mouth in mourning. How do we
       author our gentle birth, the height

we were—were we gods rolling stars across
       a sundog sky, the same as scarabs?

We fit somewhere between god
       and mineral, angel and animal,

believing a thing as sacred as the sun rises
       and falls like an ordinary beast.

Deer sniff lifeless fawns before leaving,
       elephants encircle the skulls and tusks

of their dead—none wanting to leave
       the bones behind, none knowing

their leave will lessen the loss. But birds
       pluck their own feathers, dogs

lick themselves to wound. Allow me this
       luxury. Give me tonight to cut

and salt the open. Give me a shovel
       to uproot the mandrake and listen

for its scream. Give me a face that toils
       so closely with stone, it is itself

stone. I promise to enter the flesh again.
       I promise to circle to ascend.

I promise to be happy tomorrow.

underperforming sonnet overperforming

[FOR MARILYN]

This time, this poem, is the best idea
I've ever had—the best in history
even, the best any has had, I swear . . .
and I should know, I've kept inventory
of them all; this poem is the alpha,
omega, middle, and the laterals—
literally the conceit of a far
off blank stare or a volta with virile
tendencies to talk about *it* and be
about *it*, *it* being the best sonnet
to ever *sonnet*—formal guarantees
of a good time, ready rhymes, and, I bet,
this poem is, with enormous success,
the only poem entirely imageless.

legendary

I don't want to end up an old drag queen.

OCTAVIA SAINT LAURENT

This is no primrose path, a life lived out
of boredom, a role played on occasion.
Category is fem-realness—devout
in the practice of pulling a fast one
on the eye. Octavia, eighth wonder . . .
I wonder, am I as legendary
as legend lets on? Only amateurs
are moved by monikers on a marquee.
Only amateurs imagine Harlem
leads to Hollywood. I can't afford such
idle delusions. So close I see them
flickering, but not close enough to touch.
So beautiful I almost forget, were
it not for history, to know better.

an apology for trashing magazines
in which you appear

I was out of line, Brad Pitt.

You're no Eliot Spitzer.

I'm no preacher. This apology no bully pulpit

where I sermonize our epitasis—

a Woody Allen tragicomedy in which I play "Serendipity,"

and am blinded by you, a star, Jupiter

(third brightest in the night, spitting

image of the sky god). *Patience* might be for pipits

and "forever" a spit

of land neighboring Atlantis, but I'll wait my turn. Pity

your first marriage ended. I didn't mind her as much as that Jolie-Pitt

situation, complete with pitter-

patter of 12 *Benetton*-inspired feet. But, I'm not bitter. My pit

bull bears your name, and I call my man—with whom I'm going to

   Pittsburgh

for a wedding—out his name. Into yours: Brad Pitt.

Daydreams of you and me rivaled only by Brandon and me on *Peach Pit*

counters, from the original *90210*. Even so, I'd wish he were you.

   Adonis epitome.

Abandon Hollywood for Bed-Stuy, skip down spit-paved sidewalks to my brownstone. My poetry pittance,

your movie money . . . I suspect we'd do fine with our combined

    capital.

We'd be the mixed-race Pitts

on Tompkins Park. I'd be hospitable,

hosting meet and greets so as not to appear uppity.

Casually introducing you, I'd say, "Oh, this is Brad. This is just Brad

    Pitt."

You'd find macabre humor in my obsession with Poe's *Pit*

and the Pendulum and the palpitating

Tell-Tale Heart. The heart is an odd organ, a maudlin muscle, a cesspit

of undeserved affection. I admit I've had trouble pitting

good sense against non, but who hasn't? (Did you know the per capita

divorce rate is 50%? Pitiful.)

Like with Juliette and Jennifer, I pray Angelina was a pit

stop on your way to Brooklyn. When I first saw you, Brad Pitt,

I was 15 and became so ill I was rushed to the hospital.

My hands, feet and armpits

began to sweat as if I were riding horseback up a hill toward a love

    who made the pit

of my stomach ache; literally, *Legends of the Fall* was my pitfall.

Brad Pitt, I imagine a much older you—spitfire
and only slightly decrepit—staring my epitaph
down as if your gaze were the capital and my headstone a ghetto to be
    pitied.

even the gods

Even the gods misuse the unfolding blue. Even the gods misread the windflower's nod toward sunlight as consent to consume. Still, you envy the horse that draws their chariot. Bone of their bone. The wilting mash of air alone keeps you from scaling Olympus with gifts of dead or dying things dangling from your mouth— your breath, like the sea, inching away. It is rumored gods grow where the blood of a hanged man drips. You insist on being this man. The gods abuse your grace. Still, you'd rather live among the clear, cloudless white, enjoying what is left of their ambrosia. Who should be happy this time? Who brings cake to whom? Pray the gods do not misquote your covetous pulse for chaos, the black from which they were conceived. Even the eyes of gods must adjust to light. Even gods have gods.

in defense of "candelabra with heads"

If you've read the "Candelabra with Heads"
that appears in this collection and the one
in *The Animal*, thank you. The original,
the one included here, is an example, I'm told,
of a poem that can speak for itself, but loses
faith in its ability to do so by ending with a thesis
question. Yeats said a poem should click shut
like a well-made box. I don't disagree.
I ask, "Who can see this and not see lynchings?"
not because I don't trust you, dear reader,
or my own abilities. I ask because the imagination
would have us believe, much like faith, faith
the original "Candelabra" lacks, in things unseen.
You should know that human limbs burn
like branches and branches like human limbs.
Only after man began hanging man from trees
then setting him on fire, which would jump
from limb to branch like a bastard species
of bird, did we come to know such things.
A hundred years from now, October 9, 2116,
8:18 p.m., when all but the lucky are good
and dead, may someone happen upon the question

in question. May that lucky someone be black
and so far removed from the verb *lynch* that she be
dumbfounded by its meaning. May she then
call up Hirschhorn's *Candelabra with Heads*.
May her imagination, not her memory, run wild.

instead of executions, think death erections

I wish the day hadn't.
Dawn has claimed
another sky, its birds.

I watch from my burning
stake the broken necks.
Once, this lot

allowed wildflowers—
nothing worse than bruised
wildflowers. Darling

dawn, death mask
to which I've grown
accustomed, show me

one pretty thing
no heavier
than a hummingbird.

unframed

Handle this body. Spoil
it with oils. Let the
residue corrode, ruin it.
I have no finish, no
fragile edge. (On what
scrap of me have we
not made desire paths,
so tried as to bury
ourselves therein?) I
beg: spare me gloved
hands, monuments to
nothing. I mean to die a
relief against every wall.

object permanence

[FOR JOHN]

We wake as if surprised the other is still there,
each petting the sheet to be sure.

How have we managed our way
to this bed—beholden to heat like dawn

indebted to light. Though we're not so self-
important as to think everything

has led to this, everything has led to this.
There's a name for the animal

love makes of us—named, I think,
like rain, for the sound it makes.

You are the animal after whom other animals
are named. Until there's none left to laugh,

days will start with the same startle
and end with caterpillars gorged on milkweed.

O, how we entertain the angels
with our brief animation. O,

how I'll miss you when we're dead.

notes

"Medical History": Though the last line of the poem suggests otherwise, the stars in the sky are most likely not dead. The distance between the stars and us is so great that we can only see the brightest stars, which is to say the most alive.

"Candelabra with Heads": 2006, Thomas Hirschhorn, part of the Tate Collection. The poem is written in a form created by the author called *Obverse*. The poem's second half is written in the reverse order of the first and the last line is the "thesis question" of the poem.

"Legendary" (Venus Xtravaganza): Venus Xtravaganza was an Italian American transgender performer featured in *Paris Is Burning*, a documentary film about drag pageants in 1980s Harlem.

"It's Not Fitness, It's a Lifestyle": The poem shares its title with the slogan of the luxury gym Equinox.

"The First Person Who Will Live to Be One Hundred and Fifty Years Old Has Already Been Born": The title is borrowed from "Who wants to live forever? Scientist sees aging cured," the Reuters article by Health and Science Correspondent Kate Kelland.

"In Igboland": The poem refers to the construction of an *mbari* in Nigeria. An *mbari* is a building erected in response to a major catastrophe and dedicated to one or several local deities. The majority of which are made for Ala, goddess of earth.

"Legendary" (Pepper LaBeija): Pepper LaBeija was an African American female impersonator featured in *Paris Is Burning*.

"And": The poem is inspired by Thomas Sayers Ellis's poem entitled "Or."

"Cento for the Night I Said, 'I Love You'": The poem is comprised entirely of lines borrowed from the following poets (in order of appearance): C. D. Wright, Mary Jo Salter, Patricia Smith, Toi Derricotte, Philip Levine, Lynda Hull, Langston Hughes, Malachi Black, Kimberly Blaeser, Maxine Kumin, Afaa Michael Weaver, Hédi Kaddour, dg nanouk okpik, Claude McKay, Deborah Landau, Sharkmeat Blue, George Bradley, Yona Harvey, Federico García Lorca, June Jordan, Kwame Dawes, W. H. Auden, Ana Castillo, Erica Hunt, Muriel Rukeyser, Ed Roberson, Ruth Madievsky, Thylias Moss, Gregory Orr, Yusef Komunyakaa, Elizabeth Spires, Lyrae Van Clief-Stefanon, Tim Seibles, Nathalie Handal, Wisława Szymborska, Lucille Clifton, C. P. Cavafy, Rainer Maria Rilke, Raúl Zurita, August Kleinzahler, Louise Glück, Victoria Redel, Adélia Prado, Sonia Sanchez, Jean Sénac, Claribel Alegría, Remica L. Bingham-Risher, Sylvia Plath, Harryette Mullen, Emily Dickinson, Eric Gamalinda, Galway Kinnell, John Murillo, Sharon Strange, Larry Levis, Sherman Alexie, Franz Wright, Marianne

Boruch, Andrea Cohen, Linda Susan Jackson, Carl Phillips, Robert Hayden, Eavan Boland, Anne Waldman, Dorianne Laux, Natasha Trethewey, Yves Bonnefoy, Tina Chang, David Wojahn, Nick Laird, Simone White, Catherine Barnett, Vladimir Mayakovsky, Brenda Shaughnessy, Kazim Ali, Brenda Hillman, Valzhyna Mort, Blas Falconer, Theodore Roethke, Kahlil Gibran, Rita Dove, Brigit Pegeen Kelly, Khaled Mattawa, Tracy K. Smith, Ed Skoog, Alice Walker, Pablo Neruda, Adrienne Rich, Percy Bysshe Shelley, Edna St. Vincent Millay, Aimé Césaire, Jake Adam York, Bob Kaufman, William Blake, Frank Bidart, Marilyn Nelson, Polina Barskova, Santee Frazier, Suheir Hammad, Cornelius Eady.

"Virginia is for Lovers": The poem shares its title with the tourism and travel slogan of the Commonwealth of Virginia.

"Clue": The poem is inspired by the murder mystery game of the same name.

"C ue": is an erasure of "Clue."

"Imagine Sisyphus Happy": The title is borrowed from the final sentence of Albert Camus's essay "The Myth of Sisyphus." The lines "Give me a face that toils/so closely with stone, it is itself/stone" are loosely borrowed from the essay as well.

"Legendary" (Octavia Saint Laurent): Octavia Saint Laurent was an African American transgender performer featured in *Paris Is Burning*.

"An Apology for Trashing Magazines in Which You Appear": The poem is inspired by Denise Duhamel's poem entitled "Delta Flight 659."

"In Defense of 'Candelabra with Heads'": "The Animal" refers to the chapbook *The Animal After Whom Other Animals Are Named*.

"Object Permanence": *Object permanence* is the understanding that objects continue to exist even when they cannot be observed.

Born in St. Thomas, U.S.V.I., and raised in Apopka, Florida, Nicole Sealey is the author of *The Animal After Whom Other Animals Are Named*, winner of the 2015 Drinking Gourd Chapbook Poetry Prize. Her other honors include an Elizabeth George Foundation Grant, the Stanley Kunitz Memorial Prize from *The American Poetry Review*, a Daniel Varoujan Award and the Poetry International Prize, as well as fellowships from CantoMundo, Cave Canem Foundation, MacDowell Colony, and the Poetry Project. Her work has appeared in *The New Yorker* and elsewhere. Nicole holds an MLA in Africana studies from the University of South Florida and an MFA in creative writing from New York University. She is the executive director at Cave Canem Foundation.